First
Language

Edward Kleinschmidt

First Language

The University of
Massachusetts Press
Amherst

Printed in the United States of America
LC 89–20187
ISBN 0–87023–699–7 (cloth); 700–4 (paper)
Set in Linotron Garamond No. 3 by Keystone Typesetting, Inc.
Printed and bound by Thomson-Shore, Inc.

Library of Congress Cataloging-in-Publication Data

Kleinschmidt, Edward, 1951–
    First language / Edward Kleinschmidt.
      p.   cm.
    ISBN 0–87023–699–7 (alk. paper) — ISBN 0–87023–700–4
(pbk. : alk. paper)
    I. Title.
PS3561.L3828F57 1990
811'.54—dc20   89–20187
                                                 CIP

British Library Cataloguing in Publication data are available.

for Frances Mayes
due volte

Acknowledgments

I am grateful to the editors of the following journals and
anthologies for permission to reprint here poems that first
appeared, some in earlier versions, in their publications:
The Agni Review 20 (1984): Fly by Night; *The American Poetry
Review*: Infantry; Anesthetic; *Another Chicago Magazine*: Past Living
(beyond the Power, Scope, Extent); *Anthology of Magazine Verse and
Yearbook of American Poetry, 1986–1988* (Monitor Book Co.):
December Poem; *The Berkeley Poetry Review*: The Anatomy Lesson;
Black Warrior Review: The Absence of Day; *College English*:
Grammatical Existence © 1985, Epidemic (among People) ©
1987, Echolalia © 1989, copyright by the National Council of
Teachers of English; *Concert at Chopin's House: A Collection of Polish-
American Writing* (New River Press, 1987): Recycle; *Five Fingers*:
The Other Side of the Road; *The Gettysburg Review*: Gangue; *Gnosis
Anthology of Contemporary American and Russian Literature and Art,*
vols. 1 & 2 © 1982 Gnosis Press: Migrations of the Cro-Magnon;
Iowa Review: Concordance; *Hablar, Aprender, Vivir*; *Literary Review*:
December Poem; *The Little Magazine*: Dog Walk; Organon; In Late
Afternoon as the Clock Sleeps; *Massachusetts Review*: Celebrating
Thinking; Avenues in Bloom; Mumbo Jumbo; *Mississippi Review* 15
(1987): Going; *The New Yorker*: Orchestrion; *The North American
Review*: Katzenjammer © 1987 by the University of Northern
Iowa; *North Dakota Quarterly*: Like Tulipomania; *Pennsylvania
Review*: Addendum (at the Time of His Death); *Pequod*: Dismissed;
Poet & Critic 17 (1985): The Explanation; *Poetry*: "Nothing Is But
What Is Not"; Random Panic in the U.S.A.; Tonight Insomnia;
Poetry Northwest: Arms and the Man; Arrangement in Black;
Boustrophedon; Some Problems with the Mind/Body Problem;
Poets On: On the Rue des Grands Regrets; *Seattle Review*: Rough
House; *Sonora Review*: At the Drowning Every Afternoon;
ZYZZYVA: Cicatrix.

I am also grateful to Santa Clara University for release time
and a Thomas Terry Award and to the Virginia Center for the
Creative Arts, where some of these poems were written.

Thanks to David Hamilton, Paul Jenkins, Joseph Parisi, Liz
Rosenberg, James Tate, and David Wagoner.

Contents

I

Atavism

I wouldn't know how else to proceed
Without that one unknown gene carried across
The border in my great-great-great-
Grandfather's coat pocket. It has been
Like a coal, burning from the inside through
Ash. My ancestors didn't ask for much.
They didn't throw back all the undersized fish
On their lines. They weren't interested in
Resurfacing the driveway so that successors
Would step on new land. They put quicksand
In the hourglass when it was necessary. How then
Time would lose track of its own spelling, become
Simply a dime for the bus to the beach, not
Even enough time for a return, but over,
Ended, sending in the I Quit notice before
Being fired. It would be no accident if my
Predecessors returned to these city limits as stop
Signs stippled with bullet holes, house numbers
Painted on the curbs, license plates rusting around
The edges. Actually they were all bad with figures.
Not much success with money either. They grew lettuce
In the backyard. They would say to neighbors that
The nine innings in life are not enough even if you've
Come to bat more than once. Everyone preferred
Slow ball then, before anyone knew about
DNA. My ancestors took a wagon into
Town loaded with wood and sold it on the street
Corner. It was early winter and wood
Was a necessary ingredient to bread. Don't
Ask me now what bread baked in a wood-fired
Oven smells like. Nobody in my past
Could put that taste in their wills. If I could
Wish for one recessive gene, it might
Be that. Rubbing my chilled hands together,
Coming into the kitchen, glasses fogging up, I see
Someone is bending over, looking through the isinglass
At what has been rising inevitably above the surface.

Mumbo Jumbo

When all my immediate family members have finally died,
When all have crossed the medians on
The major highways, the shrines that have been
Going up in their memory will come down.
Here are some: at Shrovetide eating smoked
Carp and complaining about the stars in
The sky that crush young children under
Their wheels. In the garden, my mother
With a hornet in her hair net. My young
Aunt tapping her death march on the kitchen
Table with her long red fingernails.
The coffins go down for miles and will
Soon be out of sight. My uncle began
His journey to hell every morning but
Never made it. Thousands of children like
Myself are trapped each day in abandoned
Refrigerators. I've read about people
Being buried in piano boxes and have
Wondered where the pianos are. The soprano
At the funeral hit the highest note ever hit.
The boy under the covered table in magic
Class "failed to materialize" later. My
Cousin who repairs shoes can't fix mine
Fast enough. All of the above see me in
The distance blue or smoky, a fencepost in the fog.
They have stayed dead. There was no mistake.

Cicatrix

It may mean something's healing: a slight wound
From the wind-up toy opened every Christmas.
Christians take a late-night snack of chocolate lions,
Not feeling allegiance to the king of anorexia. Rulers make
Their countrymen stay in straight lines even to the gallows.
No lethal objections—the law book's a paperweight
On the researcher's desk. The diced beets in the white
Sink couldn't be bleeding. They've nothing
Subcutaneous over us. We've flesh that's flushed
With the blush of blood that rushes through tissue.
And there's war. A man has an attaché of bombs
Attached to his wrist, circa 1986. He is now a
Plant that lives on air—his days in the ozone
Are dismal. (There are better cures for bad
Complexions: Think of Oedipus in a duplex,
Analyzing data on his p.c., looking for advice
From fleas to vice-admirals. He once killed
A conductor on the electric train that runs from
Tokyo to Kyoto. Now supports his divorced mother,
Tells his daughters to turn down the stereo.)
After scratching became writing, and scar tissue
From cuts became words, it was like seeing water
Through a hole in the ice. I see, you say,
Circling, encyclopedic, walking properly
Into a new thought. Always in the small
Barn next to the compost heap is a "stroke
Of genius," a new word for everyone wanting
New words. The maps in the basket need
Updating. The maps are where you've traveled,
And the basket is your body. There are words other
Than English words to say this: the roads on the maps:
Red for arteries, blue for veins. It isn't always
Easy to crisscross with a car. But you've gotten
Out that door long ago—you're walking. Your shoes
Leave a trail you can tell: Scars are the red
Leaves you use each late autumn to bank the rose bushes.

Doubt

I am in a room for this and the candles
Hissing on the sideboard are about to go out.
Not for the little oxygen but from lack of
Future wax. The house next door burned
Down last week and no doubt the masturbating
Arsonists in town thought those two sticks
They rub together would ignite. Like attracts
Like. The two lovers roll from the weeds into
The river, knowing they will float. A stone sinks,
But it couldn't very well believe anything else.
I've tried and tried and now I'm tired.
The clothes on the clothesline have dried. The water
Has wicked away quickly. Seems more than reasonable.
I don't doubt the *b* in *doubt* is silent, hesitating
Between *u* and *t,* isn't bubbling or bucking or blaming.
The flames from the burning house reached the tops of
Trees. I had to feel it to believe it. I had to see
It to believe it. I had to believe it to doubt that
It ever happened. All the arsonists will be burning
The newspapers that report the fire. They'll put their
Heads in their ovens and laugh. I don't believe I could
Keep my hand in the candle flame for long and so I
Don't try often. I hate to be disappointed.
Maybe what I'm wanting is a blast furnace—melting
Metal, casting iron, high heat that will burn everything up.

Innards

What has turned inward, gone off from
The repeating edges of the circle into
The center. What the doctors find when
They open us up: glue, the clue to
What keeps us together, from the heat
Of heart to the interest of intestine.
The rivers underground have no shore,
No delta, and perhaps they coil,
Like Yeats's gyres. In the dark of
The body, in viscera, in the
Thick slap of lung-sound, around
The clean bone—there we go night
Swimming, there is finding the way
Home by moonlight only. No maps,
Nothing so external as skin. In
Caves live bears. We love our human
Experiment of blood for blood's sake.
The doctor's sponge sops it up like a
Crust of bread in the stew pot. Going
Inward is better than going nowhere. Poke
Your finger into someone's stomach to make
Your point clearer. What goes down must
Come up, but the esophagus isn't necessarily
An elevator. The kidneys are little
Saddlebags riding on the spine, the fault
That conducts the tremors of the shaking old
Body, the shaking young body. Inside
There is nothing no longer to think about:
This is automatic matter, the thermostat,
The well into which thinking of thinking disappears.

Re-experience

If I've tried to sleep the sleep of deep poetry,
A ship into its slip at night as if it
Were itself water, I have also wanted to be
Startled from it, I've wanted the tide
Out, the ship in mud, stranded on land.
If this is a winter-turning-into-spring dream,
One that breaks up the ice I've been
Sleeping under, a deer floating on an ice floe
Down river, I know that that water
Will go only where it goes, there is no
Lack of direction and impetuousness. If
The expert fear, the long nights of dying
In dream only, the intimate underlining
Of my name in some book of death—I'm
Dreaming I'm turning the explicit page—
Should carry over into day, what good
Is thinking of the experience of a one-time
Death? If the interpreter of experience
Confesses that he was wrong, if trying
Again, negotiating for better dreams,
Is oppressive, then I can stop trying to
Write my way out of dark rooms. And if as
A child I loved the word *Euphrates,* and
Would now like to know the goodness of
Crossing over that river again and again, and
If now that word has disappeared, is
At this moment flowing into sand, then
Has the experiment failed, has the dry
Dream of walking across again and again
Been real, been the experience that I've lived for?

Cancerismo

This is a gut reaction to trouble. They've
Rubberbanded the lobsters' claws at Safeway.
People stare into the aquarium, not feeling any
Safer. Lately, many of the men I've seen with
Their shirts off at the local beach seem ripe
With cancerismo. Top heavy with cancer, gathering
Up cancer coins as if there were places to
Spend them. My father put his mother's welcome
Mat at the foot of her grave. He's planted
Plastic red flowers in real black dirt. They last
Even longer, he feels. It isn't reasonable to
Believe in metastasis. I've heard that to have
Transition in life, it's necessary to look down
From every bridge you cross and imagine you've
Not fallen. Although I now believe the corpse
Is truly dead. Although I've seen my grand-
Mother cry cancer cells. She would have been
Comfortable on the davenport we bought with her
Insurance money. I think I have enough red
Corpuscles to get me out of here. The doctor's
Lips are hermetical. Down the hall, someone is
Hollering, perhaps in training to be a poet.
When you get right down to it, kneeling before
Nihilism is no joke. But any ism isn't only cult for
Cult's sake. The hermit crab goes home to his shell.
The scarecrow in the field, for example, would
Be nothing without a good strong stick in the ground.

Boustrophedon

Whereas some poems are baskets catching falling
Things, some line up for the diving board
To add twenty-five laps to their scorecards.
This is such a poem. This is the turn this poem
Has taken. If the title is misleading, it is not
Meandering. Its point, like the needle's,
Only indicates direction to the doubled
Thread it is pulling. It might close up random
Pieces of cloth. Stitching can be satisfying
In itself. Take the anklebone broken from
Stepping in a pothole—it is mending and deserves
A crutch. When the bone ages a million years
It will be a prize for those looking. I have
Zigzagged up hills. I have read it is recommended.
Which is zig and which zag I am confused about:
How long can I zig—or zag—before zig loses
Its meaning and becomes, simply, straight line?
I would like to think I could zag all day, zag
To the mailbox, zag to the flowershop, zag home.
I have worn a furrow to the window and have three
Furrows in my forehead when I am surprised at what
I see. I do not know what the ox in the field
Is thinking, plowing on Sunday, twenty-five turns
It has memorized—better to be here than at the hecatomb!
These U-turns, returns, pull the line, turn, turn the world.

And Then I Woke Up

But I can't clearly remember what it was
I dreamed. Was it the right dream for that
Night or not? I would never elect to dream
About claws, for example, the way someone like
T. S. Eliot might. Yes, I've been a "thinking
Stone" in bed—the cave's cool where the wine's
Kept. I've, too, been in rooms empty except
For their temperatures. And I'd rather hit with
Hit-or-miss than not miss or not hit. It's 9:39—
Whether ante meridiem or post is not obvious in this
Poem. But through the curtain is light the window lets
In or out. It seems I was stealing through the rooms
Of Ferdinand Marcos's house in Hawaii. This was
An action dream. Usually I'm pushing a half-empty
Shopping cart down the frozen foods aisle, reading
Completely the shopping list, reading the label
On the can in my hand. Either this, or sitting in
A familiar chair, in a room, alone, reading the newspaper,
Wondering, at times, if this is what I really should
Be doing in a dream. No one comes in. There is no one
Here to leave. I'm not deceived by these. In the morning,
In the refrigerator, there's nothing new. The newsprint
Stains on my fingertips will always be there. Marcos
Might not be wandering the rooms of *my* house
(He doesn't sleep much). Waking up is not hard
To do. One eye opens, then another. The rest is history.

Infantry

Witness the big baby crying at the front line.
His highchair has toppled over like a water
Tower. Our knapsacks are stuffed with Gerber
Baby food although we're not in love with
Strained prunes. No one here ever gets beyond
The preface in most books—the war
Going on that we hate we have tried not
Speaking to, but it rolls us over like
We have rolled over soldiers to see if
They were dead, to look at their peaceful,
Horrible faces. We would want to love
Our parents to death. We have a drive
Like no one since Oedipus. How innocent
Were the little battles over buttered toast
At the kitchen table. We couldn't speak
Unless spoken to. How could we learn
To use such a word as *ineffable* in such a
Plate glass silence? If paradise is any
Garden or playground surrounded by clay walls,
It long ago received the balm of napalm.
By the way, the infantry needs clothes
A size larger, since it's growing into
Them faster. Fate is fame. In other languages,
It's hunger. When others speak *for* you,
Instead of *to* you, you know they're looking
In mirrors. Shatter that glass and cover
Your ass. You'll get a reputation. You'll
March through the arches in April, at
One point in history a cruel month. But nothing
Fatal. Even cold clean death isn't written.

Hablar, Aprender, Vivir

If I said there's a guarantee
The wash will dry in the sun

Today, the words were learned
Words, like promises of new

Lives after old lives have
Been bleached and slapped

And twisted into shapes they
Were never meant to be. Speaking

Seriously is like driving a car
Seriously—appreciation by a few

Passengers: enough. I heed stops,
Yield, remember rules glued in

Memory. I don't always know
The wet paint is wet until I touch it.

What I don't learn in school has much
To be said about it. Then why not

Speak up, over the radio waves
Tumbling the dry air. I speak like

Exposed brick under stucco, sometimes.
Or thick stew, or crumbled cheese.

Speak for the hard-luck lookers-on.
Escape hatch. Hull of the unfinished ship.

Rabbit hutch. Someone else's echo is
Most marvelous—I can think it's

Mine if I want. The want of need's lack.
Come clearly into the forest so

I can see you. You who speak, learn
The steps, live through these days.

Anesthetic

Your body obeys, under anesthesia, audible
Sighs, face following the apparent path
Of the sun. You want to take back. You
Take back. The backdrop hasn't changed between
Act One and Act Five. What was it you
Bought over the counter that you're now unhappy
With? You won't pay the ransom for
The recovery: No one's here to collect, no
Ushers walking the aisles with beechwood baskets,
Asking. There isn't a clue the rescue of sensation
Will succeed. Sensation is the réseau upon
Which any lace in your life is sewn. So, when
That's unraveled, nothing's left. Your
Center is the pinprick the compass made, tracing
A circle on the wall where the stovepipe
Goes. The smoke promptly goes up,
An example of what smoke is, where up is.
And with the eccentrics, who don't play in
The playgrounds, park in the parks, swim
In the swimming pools—don't use *them*
As examples of what's wrong. They're not cutting
Coupons, pasting pages of stamps in a book,
Flipping through catalogs at the redemption
Center for premiums. Instead, they're centrifugal,
Which isn't what I'm saying you should be.
You're too much the centerboard for the boat
That would rather be drifting, that wants to
Obey tides and currents, ending up on rocks,
If that kind of mass attracts them. You're not
Exempt simply because you don't believe.
There's no such thing as vintage belief.
Start next time, like your car starting in the morning,
After having spent all night under stars we don't
Have to see to believe they are there, samples, exemplary.

II

The Death of Adam

You were what was spun out on the first
Turn of the lathe. An awkward wooden figure
In the garden, falling into the narcissus
With loneliness. Madam, I'm Adam, you
Introduced yourself, after an afternoon nap, after
A surgical sex. There are now more
Eves than leaves. Cains can cut up the mutton.
And Abels run the grain elevators. That truck
That rumbles over your grave stirs up a ton
Of dust. Remember: Dropped fruit is best
If you don't happen to own the tree. There has since
Been an evolution in taste, for being bid
By the forbidden is old-fashioned. There's no
Fruit sweet enough not to sin for and ladders
Are a good substitute for things spiritual.
Macadamia nuts need a twenty-ton
Press to be split open. They are a
Metaphor of their own philosophy. I can see
You in your last days, eight or nine
Hundred years old, a cowboy mending
Fences to keep in a few head of kosher beef.
Or you'd be plowing up arrowheads
And then quickly hiding this kind of evidence.
You were proud of being proto-, the *Ubermensch*
Who said, I sin, therefore I am. Although
You *were,* as we at present are, as we
Whirl off into this present fad of dying.
If you've developed the phallic side of
Your personality, you know, too, that you're
Unregenerative, a bad reaction to a first
Cause. Death is one of the consequences
Of believing too much in the future.
Have you finished what you've started?
Would you like to shake out the braids in
Your beard like a young girl's hair?
Does the cane you walk with enable
You to go freely to the spring that

Flows miraculously from the split rock?
You could not imagine mass graves ringed
With olive trees, fossils turned into relics.
When the seed that Eve planted under your tongue
Germinated, it sent roots far away from the sun.

Recycle

Every day I say that the last day coming
Around again is gaining. Not overtaking,
But overreaching, like the Encyclopedia Sale.
Fallow fields are always next in line
For cultivation. Soon the colonists arrive,
Inhabit the hell out of the soil, with
Their reinvented wheels. There'll come a time,
There'll come a time. Right now the helmsmen
Seem oddly overwhelmed, washed overboard.
The cyclamen out front are waving their red
Ripped flags. Draw a line at the point of no return:
I'll be there, high on the list, or low-down,
Somersaulting, pedaling like mad, looking forward.

Concordance

An understanding of the past has set us back:
In our terraplane, throttle wild, what we see

Is what was dead. The spearhead flying in our minds
Retreats from the open field to the sepulcher where

The flowers planted take on their own life just once,
Show their life as single notes of an English horn

That is planted in our minds in a different, an
Abstract, way. Music, especially sepulcher music,

Is abstract and ordinary. The lichen covers the grave-
Stones like words cover a page. We read them like

First graders, balancing the mystery on the tip
Of our finger: What we can pronounce is ours. What

We cannot, we pass to the one behind us, a process of
Extremes, small but opposite. An *avocet* is a small

Extreme of a *pelican:* Neither is musical except for
Its name. One has a needle-beak, the other a mailpouch.

They are everything birds can be in their present moments.
Their pasts might tell them to ignore the albatross,

Avoid loud parties and some Italian mussels, follow
Out to sea any promising rusty barges. In the sand,

We are the terrible children playing with our whizzbangs.
When in doubt we look up, look down, smile, or hold on.

We have little in relation to these birds except the past,
A symbol on our tombstones, a wing slicing a piece of sky.

On our own private beaches, which we inexplicably share,
If we must pass notes to each other, let them be musical.

Echolalia

The parrot next door isn't purring. That's
The cat's job, motor turned on when hand
Brushes face. The parrot talks to the self
Shining in the linoleum floor, scuff marked
And waxed, wanting to be thick red tile in
Spain. New rain has fallen again. About
Time, the cat isn't thinking now in the garden,
The last garden, the one that followed the first
Garden so quickly. The potatoes were so unlike
The celery, as if at any minute they could
Change, both of them, into nothing, or nothing
We'd immediately recognize, and so forget
Immediately. Like hand brushing cat's face so
Absently. Sounds like a miracle, the true
Reflection in a mirror. A bird in the desert rides
On the sound waves made by the big trucks on
The interstate. The fly swallowed alive by the cat
Flies up the windpipe, suffocating in the stomach.
In San Francisco, there are no bats to feed on the bugs
That aren't here. Like attracts hate, to trap it.
When I dropped the pen on the floor just now, I
Thought of it stopping in mid-fall, writing a word
In the air, the last writing before a new
Life. Sadly, a drop is that which is squeezed
Out, leaving nothing but pulp, pulp of
Pumpkin, for example, what is left from
The first seed. We have yet to know where
Light is located. My brother always asks me
To point to my mind and I'm still standing
Here statuesque. Slight variation of squawk
Is what I hear now from the parrot. He's
Imitating the garbage disposal, the industrial
Park, nuclear power, the dust under the refrigerator.
Repeat after me is a line I've heard. Writing it
Is different. It's like the wind writing your name
In the grass—nobody has really ever spelled it that way.

Some Problems with the Mind/Body Problem

First, why is it always mind/
Body, one, two, why not body/

Mind, one, two? For example,
Peter's painful ache in his

Toes must have told his mouth
To form the painful word: gout.

How else could he have known?
Or: Ludwig Wittgenstein's

Large brain sorted out Bach
Like a chest of drawers. His

Brother, Paul, had Ravel write
A concerto for his one hand,

Left. Therefore, if the brain-
Pan is cracked, the body

Might think it's a horse not
Being led to water, at all.

Some solutions that haven't worked:
Exercise for the mind to lose

Weight, to feel lighter, not
So heavy-handed, so leadfooted.

My uncle had his wooden leg
Cremated with his real body.

A reasonable man, he could talk
For hours about phantom pain.

And finally, when my father brought
A burlap sack of chickens home, my

Mother would boil water for plucking.
In the alley, I would wait

For the headless bodies to come
Running into my arms. Their

Heads, combs quivering, in
The grass—beaks like scissors

With no paper to cut. The bodies
So aimless, shot out clots of blood.

This is a clear-cut case. In all
Problems there must be some connection.

Celebrating Thinking

Walking your dog to the gold mine out back,
You form a word and drop it down the shaft.
The party last night with uninvited guests
Destroyed the glasses, vases, double beds.

You think that maybe one or two old friends
Cannot tell lies, not even if they're paid
Huge sums, given fast cars, patted on the back,
Or roughed up, exiled, thrown to sharks.

Nonsense. A dream flew by, a bigger dream
Than most, and stayed awhile, longer than
You cared. The trouble with shadows knocking
Over expensive china is you can't collect.

A nuisance to be known as a fool, especially when
Fools aren't valued, aren't given an outlet for
Their calling. You'll survive, live like a boat on
The water, sell rain to the natives, tape your laughter.

About thinking: when a thought hits you, let it run,
Walk, crawl, stand still, be a thought, itself, whatever.
When you're looking to think, though, walk backward,
Squint, climb flagpoles, build fires, sleep, have a drink.

Organon

Take two drops under the tongue
For every day you're awake,

You will reawaken, you will shine.
It doesn't matter that the words

Aren't where you want them, words
Drift, words jump ship, words can't

Keep track of themselves for long.
Throw out proof as soon as you

Sense it, it won't stand up in
The world. Sew conjecture into

The lining of your jacket, pad your
Shoulders, push your ideas out

That pastry tube, arrange the sweet
Peas in their defensive position, and

Smile, you'll win the argument, you'll
Pass the test. When the requirements

Call for egg whites, stiff and
Stubborn, keep that copper bowl

Going, you're against the clock
All wound up. Know science, but

Know your subject. Stop defending
Matter if you can't point to

Something that points back. There
Is cause for those crazy to go

Crazier, it has to be, it's in
The works. But the tape recorder

Clicked off and you're still
Talking! How can you believe

You're right. You should play
Back the last part, where you dive

Through little hoops because you want
To, where you seem to forget the reason.

Nominalists

They wash their clothes in well water
And wear them wet and the clothes cling
Throughout the morning then hang loosely,
Lovely, white. Color is a name,
A domino theory, light
That tells them go eat, go bathe,
Go sleep, do something before another
Change occurs. Accuracy is what
The target tells the arrow from afar.
See nominalists shoot holes through the fabric:
Manufacturing good men, good women, them-
Selves included, making do, marching
In March. They seem casual about their
Cause because the case they say they
Make is this: take a case of wine,
Inside there are bottles, and inside them is wine,
And so on. They anticipate the red light
But don't count on it. Stopping gives
Them no extra trouble. Or they go right
On going. The gong is in the gong, the bell
Rings the bell, this is this, yes we know.
They fill up the vase with water,
Then flowers. Rivers flow. Perhaps
The bedsheet off the bed is
Something they hadn't counted on. With
Their razors they slice their wrists in
The warm bath water—they know that death
Cannot be replastered and hung with fresh
Paintings. This is not a job for nominalists,
Who would rather not be naming names.
So harangue or not, these bells ring
Bells. Candles want to be blown out or
They can do no good. Nominalists blow—
It's their one betraying act, whatever
Word they form as they watch
The candles go very suddenly out.

Dog Walk

When it is late, so late the clock sneezes in the cold,
And this alley has on a coal miner's hat, the words

We whisper to each other become the chipped white bone
Of our animal language. When we are tired, the way

An ocean liner sails in a photograph, we think of thin trees,
Or a 17th-century Japanese painting of rain. The moon

Slows down, limp and homogenized. We feel traced over,
An outline with the light shining behind us. Then the smoke

Too is burning. We feel we are limited to having three
Working bones in our bodies. Our skin takes on the taste

Of sand. We have to break into the safety of bridges,
And then stay there, our way out cut off: when a dog

Walks across our path, we turn into the side streets,
Which waver like the nervous, decorative lines of a bird's wing.

At the Drowning Every Afternoon

Later I can cram myself
Into the sleep box, that

Steamy sweat box, think of
The wood—burnt flesh of

Oak—for the dream trunk.
I pack well when I travel, take

Nothing. Write nothing. Write
Nothing home, or to friends, who

Should just know anyway, if they're
Friends. I ride the rental cars,

Take the trolleys to the beach.
In my bag of plums, the pits

Rattle, the peaches bruise.
These are not aimless

Fruits, they've done with their
Hanging time. Here are some

Apples so hard that they
Ache. But the sand is soft,

The sand is soft. If swimming were
Like writing with innumerable strokes:

Make an N into an M,
Toss a line to an O and

It's a Q, it's quick, it's understandable,
It's giving something new. The story

I was dreaming when the legs I use
For walking turned to stone turned

To stone. That's how I've spent these
Last ten years, trying to memorize what

Happened right before: before the fish
Net and the rock fish laughing, in

Their cups at the bottom, with fresh
Cod pulling lines like butler's bells,

And my mother said, Wear an overcoat,
It's cold, and the rowboat with

Its whale ribs, water belly, after
Birth, I'm always given one more chance.

Gangue

When the floors, the walls, the windows in
This room shake, it could mean the train,
The earthquake, the neighbors. Plaster is
The last up, first to fall, having cracked from
Ceiling to baseboard. Then it is patched, painted to
Match. In the curtain at the opera is an opening the actors
Walk through for applause. They come out, they go
Back in. The orchestra stands and we see a sea
Of heads. The playing was loud enough, the singing
Was loud enough, too. If there is confusion
Later, in the parking garage among cars, cars
Must have their own time. They speed home, tires on
Smooth road, half the clocks on the dashes working.
I've walked the hypotenuse of the trapezoid piazza in
Pienza. There is no space left in Siena's Duomo to
Carve one's initials, the floor already completely
Covered with graffiti. I've thrown confetti *con brio.*
I've clapped at flocks of pigeons flapping around
Towers. I've waxed the tile floor until the squares
Became diamonds. I've preferred tree houses over non-
Tree houses. The brush fire out of control has been
Contained. If time is a stoppered bottle, I am
A bucket. The camera clicks and goes on to the next
Picture. I've lived, mostly, in wood-frame houses,
Except for one stone farmhouse. And one root
Cellar for one summer. Renting from a landlord
Seems feudal and is only missing a little machicolation
Or a moat. The suicide note so-and-so left
In the car had some great lines. In the paint
Factory, all the paint was red.
The doctor threw his patient's vocal cords in the dumpster.
The earthquake increased the size of his property.
There was a fissure all down his throat.
We have words like crack, buzz, and ring
And cracked, buzzed, and rang. These are noises
That disappear when I cover my ears.

III

Tonight Insomnia

Hits like some knee in
The *boules d'amour*, as Flaubert

Named them. Shatters safety
Glass where I'm not cut but

Can't go 60 m.p.h. anymore, the wind
Drying my eyes to black beans.

A truck outside becomes the truck
Inside that backs up with its warning

Bell gonging. And two members
Of my high school gang dead ten

Years now in a high speed chase.
The speed in my arteries is twice

That in my veins, my heart feels
Radioactive. I'm wearing X-ray

Glasses, but I still can't see what's
Holding up this house from falling

Down, like the minute hand falling,
Struggling up to number 12.

I'm restless, it's four in
The morning, my eyes are

Green awake in this dark blue
Room. I dreamed earlier of walking

Downstairs, in the pink refrigerator
Light seeing my mother and

Grandmother eating cold potatoes
From the same bowl. I had not

Seen them in twenty years.
This is a simple dream. I don't

Like the graveyard shift any more
Than anyone does. Eye masks, ear plugs,

Gloves and socks, nose plugs, taped
Mouth—none of these works well. Now,

I remember that young doctor I discovered
In the rec room at 3 a.m. years ago

Piecing together a black jigsaw puzzle
Given earlier that day to his dead patient.

Going

Going not like guns going off but
Songs going off tongues, singers not
Wondering what's next but singing,
And young girls whirling into the dust
Of the backyard that had been snow covered,
Below zero, stopping. The blind man follows
The clothesline with his hand, wet wash dripping
On his chest. His only guests for the last forty
Years were the five ghosts of his children. The car
Stops at the top of the hill and everyone piles out.
The bridge goes on into the fog, lights blinking.
They come, and they go to sleep, stopping only to dream.
And the boats they are dreaming of go silently over
Water the dreams continue to supply without stopping.

Random Panic in the U.S.A.

In the backyard
You were clipping

Your toenails in the sun.
A dog was barking

At a butterfly. The wind
Had collapsed on your

Doorstep. You don't button
Your collar anymore.

The plastic
Chair is baking on

The hot patio stones.
You are by yourself,

Not beyond. I would
Look through the keyholes

In your house, but
They're stuffed with cotton

From aspirin bottles. As
For the sun, protect

Yourself from it.
Go inside, crawl

Under your bed and
Cry, if you must.

The dust isn't bad;
It won't kill you,

Your mother said,
Your mother told you

Every day of *her* life.
She was wrong. She

Had a black road
Where her blood ran.

She gave you random
Thoughts in a basket

For your wedding. You
Burnt them but you wanted

More. Now she's dead and
The pans need relining

And the pictures need
To be hung. In the hot

Sun, the waves of heat
Wash over you. The heat

Balloons the words you
Think into thoughts that

Are beyond your reach.
Cross to your garden.

Carry on. Dig a weed
Out. Think about potatoes,

Wet and bulbous, under
All this. The day will

Soon collect in the
Corners of your patio.

Brew the coffee, find
The smells that keep

Coming from somewhere
In your house. When

You find them you will know
What to do, you will know.

December Poem

How beautiful the dark, loose, ripe, glossy daylight comes
Without surprise. As if "to startle" meant to dart
Inward, grab what's to be had there, return full and
Ready. For what, the last month? Cold water, hard ground, half-
     bright air?
The short days stay like the others: like they've come from
The country house, back to where artificial light
Happens without success, fulfillment. Take the streets,
For example, indiscreetly bright. Crowded, too.
It seems as if more should be seen in this last act
Of every first year. But perhaps white rooftops hide
The audience, disguise it even to itself:
Gray light, an engraving we wish we could erase.

The Absence of Day

Day is no neighbor
To night but the distant
Cousin swimming in the flooding
River. We can recognize her
By her clothes that don't
Fit as she dries off
On her pontoon. At noon
At her kiln she glazes
Terra-cotta fish. At three
She leaves her shadow
On the wooden planks of the dock
And dives, coming up for air
At five, dragging out
The hours after her.
Earlier, at six, she picked
The leaves from the mulberry
Tree for dye and her hands
Became deep red, and at
Eight in the light the weight
Of things was lessened: She
Took away from the dark accumulated
From the night before. By ten
There were ten things clearer
To every one there had been
Before. And so it was.
She now runs the night ferry service
To the peninsula, to all the islands.

Dismissed

Ought I not walk to what I want that
I know won't worry you somehow?
Secretly, you are casual, not in a negative
Way. The plan of most cities is regimented,
A thought blocked out and realized,
Seen by you at every corner, every
Street you choose not to cross. But
Consider this mistake: you know someone
Well, okay? Now, one moment later, you
Don't, all right? And then, again, you
Do, fair enough? You have done this, this
Is normal. Should I not, though, can
I not, please, would it be too much if I
Asked for something from you that you
Haven't had yet, that you tell me isn't there?

Avenues in Bloom

The blind can be blind
When there is no reason to be:

Seeing to the end, the pin-
Point, the center of the flowers.

The smells are unlit chandeliers of
Finches and swallows, or the autobus

Wheels crushing yellow narcissus
Into dust. Blessed be the pictures

Of hyacinths, but they are poor
Copies, and the painters reap

The scent. Some roadside roses
Are dying, sucking at their

Straws, and there's only sound
At the bottom of the glass. Some

Flowers shout back at their vendors
When they leave, clutching the bare

Arms of an American, or riding on a
Mexican's head. Black truck

Smoke coughs in all our faces—
Kills flowers, kills humans.

Raffle of flowers, long rich
Chance for the blindmen to ride on.

Arms and the Man

At ease soldiers in
Peace sit on their

Bullets. Nothing to
Joke about. No

Harm done. Some
Take pot shots from

Their green jeep at
The armadillo in

The rocks. The spiral
Inside their gun

Barrel spins the shiny
Shell, ringing in the road,

Thumping into cactus. Planes
Above drop men below.

Rain for the picnic. Bombs
For the bomb shelter. Casual

Sex can once again be
Casual if there's no

Patrol tonight, no grinning
Grenade of teeth to bite

Off legs. What's life
Without an active

Minefield in a field of
Poppies and daffodils? Why

Not be delirious when a
Million men back every move

You make? Why not move
And take, then take and

Take and take? Your wars
Are domestic arts in

Killing right bodies,
The civilians of love, food,

Sun, and night. No honor
But in death, and then not.

We'll meet. Death is
The strangest introduction.

Addendum (at the Time of His Death)

Just let me add that. That the hat
In the closet I've never worn will
Be tossed into the ring of someone
Else's life. I've watched my cat,
Who was caught in the barn fire
Last year, grow a new coat of black
Hair. She would sleep on wet towels
And lick her pink skin until it bled.
This datum still dazzles me: the fuzz
That first covered her body. Let me
Just add that as I lived my life
As a translator, there was little
More that I wanted to do but betray
Tradition. Not be a *bad* traitor,
But trade the past for the present
And call it even. Added to my
Last morning, I'd like a little
Afternoon, just a few hours until
Late afternoon or early evening, or
A few more to mid-evening to
Good night, or just a morning like
This morning, nothing much out
Of the ordinary. The cat has stopped
Shivering. Some obituaries have pictures
Of the dead, although rarely is there
A follow-up article, meaning flesh
Is one-way, no U-turns. Just
Let me add something I should have
Added. The coat I got for my birthday
Is in the hall closet. It's never been
Worn. I would almost want to be wrapped in it.

On the Rue des Grands Regrets

Dry lipped, in your own desert of man-
Made tears, crow about your largest
Fear: the sun not setting on your
Fresh cut grave. If the distance

Between love and let's not love is
Even greater than a handspan, your
Earth would not quake, the mirror
Would say ho-hum back at you. You

Wish for an avalanche of oranges—
Just this once, for *me* you say, to
Out-set the sun, or the tropical fish
Zooming past the skin diver's eyes.

You were born thirty years ago, you have
Sixty more to go—count them down to
Nothing, use your fingers, watch them
Drop away. Lose ten here, there, burn up

Ten watching smoke rising from chimneys,
Another five walking the same route,
Three waiting for the loud busses up
The slow hill, four wishing you were dead,

Four wishing you were alive, two being
Grateful, one hateful, one sipping coffee,
One or two dying. The movie of your life
Is the one you walked out on (after sneaking

In the exit) and crossed the street to a bar,
Smoked your last pack of cigarettes, two at
A time. Your lungs were little flares of
Distress. Now you smoke pencils and write

With the ash. Now you open windows and
Shout at the crowds gathering below. You
Take a boat out on the ocean and
The fishermen wave their heavy nets at you.

Your hotel life is not bad—you are simply
Rereading something you had underlined
In a college textbook: *they started with-*
Out him and noticed that he never arrived.

"Nothing Is But What Is Not"

Hinged to some kind of door, for example,
The trap door at center stage where the ghost
Disappears. An invisible key goes into an
Invisible lock to open it. There are other
Are not's: the space in the concave spoon,
The moon in the blind dog's eyes, the ice-
Making machine unplugged. The have-nots wonder
About halving what the haves have. Why not?
No one seems to be sitting in the empty
Chair. No one has been in the saloon. Picture
The picture frames in the gallery. I have
Thought; that is to say, I have said. And
In between all was gap, and then stop-gap.
If I've spent past time nothing-ing, there'll be
Less of this in the future. What about that hole
You've been digging to China, I've been asked.
And I've had to reply—it's going nowhere.
We all have to hope the train will reappear
From the tunnel, its existence preceding
Its essence, which is all smoke to begin with,
Or end with. Nothing is ever left hanging for very long.

Migrations of the Cro-Magnon

There are now one hundred of us
And we are fascinated that we have

Become celebrities in so short a time.
Of course we have been given things:

Five-sided arguments, recycled eyeglasses
And false teeth, bookstores no one has been in

For years, abandoned brownstones.
When we gallop, we are large white

Trunks of bodies, forgetting propriety,
And without a sad thought for the passing

Landscape. In the sunlight we are happy
To have shadows to pull out of our pockets

And inflate. An event like the earth sinking
Beneath our shoes is troubling,

But trouble isn't news to live by.
Our society has all the finality

Of a window latch clicking into place.
Obviously, there is a small amount

Of bravery available, the kind found
Shivering in damp clothing. But

With the drought on the freeway,
With signs too close to the eyes,

We've hidden the blurred negatives
And have gone away to live again.

Arrangement in Black

What has happened What swings
Or crashes What such trouble
What care What walnuts we
See What kind What pears
Not picked What matter of
Fact What summer ended What
Next What pencil scratch
Whatever What time on
The farm What father What is
Dead in the dreams last night
What comes alive just through
Breathing What face blown up
What face puffed out What exterior
Lung What violent time What unknown
What smiles from the dead What
Did he know What the end
What kind What is gone What
Sinks around his shoes What long
Fingers What disappears What tells
The time What ends again What sleeps
What dies What when the sheets
Creep up together What when they
Are as long as his body will ever be
What room What smell What color
What if the windows darken
Behind the curtains What sky
Not in the room What light What
Sound of light What can the mirror
Over the bed do What talk now
What singing What sound What walking

Rough House

The axe-men swing black axes to crack the oak
Trunks in the back field, field full of flat
Stumps and sawdust from the saw's teeth.
Forget the tops of trees, they've toppled,
Crushed the mint, created groundswells,
Rushed through air, a traffic of branches.
Then flat boards squeeze out of trees, released
From a roundness they had been becoming, turn
Long linear feet, are fastened and hastily become
House. Now the builders are rough breathing
Like Greeks, saying house (of unknown origin).
They know the sounds of nails pounding at the doors,
Paint poured on the primed floorboards, shouts of
Home, not broken up, but carefully, carefully cut.

IV

Medication

I trust that the croutons aren't burning. Down-
Stairs someone's playing *Dies Irae* over and over on the sax-
Ophone, and most people who call my answering machine
Leave nothing but questions. Last summer in the center
Of the Pantheon, I thought of my pancreas, tucked under
My stomach, secreting secretly the insulin that insulates
Me from the diabetes beading up on my father's forehead.
It's fortunate I don't live above a tuba player—that
Would be it. It would be spending the night erasing the foot-
Prints I made during the day. It would be Dialing For
Deities, asking that the cash flow start flowing. When
The sax begins "Pennies from Heaven," I leave. Visit
My brother, who is having a bad day. We sit quietly in his
Big black car, waiting for a spot in the underground
Garage. He has sprayed his windows with deicer.
Afterward it is afternoon, not yet time to go moonlighting,
But getting closer. Pluto as a planet is as far away
As it will ever be. In front of the Opera House go
A diva and her divus, practicing urban verbs. They are
Atoms to each other, not divisible. They are divine and
Shape their own ends. One is Giga, 10^9, and the other is
Nano, 10^{-9}. They are looking for their next meal: It will
Soon be time to eat. Today is modern: There are more
Microseconds in a minute than minutes in the 20th Century.
A train goes by on schedule, clicking the rails, cowcatcher
Shoveling snow. The ticking of the conductor's pocketwatch is
Louder in the tunnel. In town the crowds cross at the walk
Signs, half-speed for half-life, full speed for full. I think of
The short and long days of Lent, the twelve pills my father
Takes, the hour I was born divided by the hour I will die. Have
The irrigation ditches been opened? Will there be an endless run
Of dry summers? Will the house across the street stand
Longer than the house across the street? I don't know, I keep
Telling my brother, who hasn't moved from the driver's seat,
Nor has the car moved. At the theater last night he says
There was a doctor in the house who left through the back door.

In Late Afternoon as the Clock Sleeps

The maestro cuts his radishes into rosettes,
Thinking, "who will understand this language
And its roots?" Does the cerebellum profit

From things antebellum—a cello
With gut strings witnessing a hanging?

This is surprising to the maestro. His ears
Fizz in their juices. He
Bastes his heart—his last hope

Browning evenly. A shadow drops by
And starts laughing at the chandelier.

An usher hushes the dusky intruder.
The wall clock is innocent, shy, unlike
The maestro's mind, delirious after breaking

Out of its cellophane wrapping. His proud eyes
Sweep the clean country of the kitchen and look at
The clock—a peaceful ox, its sharp domestic horns sleeping.

The Explanation

The desire to be found in spring
Under large leaves wanting sun

Is fanned by three o'clock winds
Serving to cool our bodies and breaths.

All night, the furnaces fill with wine.
We only come up to grab more air.

The grapes lie like clusters of moons
In the lyric-white bowl. The world is

Turning with the wind and the wind
Is catching itself turning with the world.

The explanation is like a flash of lightning
Half in love with the ground it strikes.

The blue sky towers over us as if,
And the clocks stumble through the doors.

If we could surprise some cure for time
Or even grab the light and toss it in the trunk,

The rest would be easy, back to desire again,
And the drugged guards would surrender the keys.

Past Living (beyond the Power, Scope, Extent)

Through an open window lives plain matter, backward and
    Forward and in between. Father was a boy until
Twenty then died and married and started farming. Returns
    From the grave are no turns between four and six—some
Turn, line of horns behind them. If life were lived out in
    An oak barrel, we'd have less wine with dinner.
Twenty is a twin to any number; doubled it's more or less.
    In triple time we watch the plants in the hot
Sun drop quickly. Any argument against time is worthwhile
    Listening to. And any trouble getting into (that
Is worth it) can't be sold or given away. Father's past is
    A crowbar rusting in a corn field.
Who put it there is an obvious question and an answer might be
    In the corn crib. A common
Experience on the farm is jumping and diving in the hay barn—
    Hay is hollow and light like cows.
The tractor pulls the traffic up the long hill. The
    Stoplights stop their business. Everyone is idle.
Twenty, forty, sixty, eighty, one hundred chickens, cows,
    Pigs, cats, dogs will not line up to be counted.
Give each a name and count the names. Take the best to the
    Fair. Put the pig's feet in the vinegar,
The cow's tongue on a hook in the smokehouse, the headcheese
    Stewing in cast iron, the cock's comb floating in beet soup.
The mind, from ten feet away, seems to disappear, is shadow
    Of sorrow, thoroughly misunderstood,
Misunderstanding. A piano, meandering in the parlor, under
    The steam of fingers it seems to know, seems to
Move out of shadow. Father's mind leaves a trail in order
    To backtrack, backlog, backward, backwoods.
The farm is thick in white clay, gets in mouths and noses,
    Spit white. The chickens are clouds of dust
On the ground—no rain. The corn is bursting the boundaries
    Of juice. Everything is baked on, white
Porcelain but not, a ruddiness bleached out, scattered white
    Flowers, white floured hands on the rising dough.

The last segment of Father's time is short. A quarter-inch
    Long wick. Puffballs. A little breath of wind,
A little salt on the bluejay's tail. The river twists its own
    Sayings and has to be believed. The blackberries
Are crushed into his hands, juice dripping into a glass, the
    One beside his bed, the one always, even now, empty.

Epidemic (among People)

The blue gaze is everywhere.
The roosters down below made a sound

That was like their name, accordion at
The cockfight, flute of prostitutes.

Arms and legs are snakes shedding their skin,
Snakes wrapped around cracked water glasses.

Down below, the bellows of the dull
Afternoon sucks in a few trees standing

Alone in the landscape. Their names
Are swing, bark, run, hide, and get lost.

Friday night hollows out the shallow
Caves on the cliffs. By morning these

Pockets are stuffed with the orphans who
Always think there is room, especially

After the war has killed so many. On corners,
For sale and selling: cans of candles,

Cradles full of rocks, a chandelier on fire,
A lottery ticket for the chance that you

Won't be here tomorrow. Four more
Gorgeous stars after thinking they

Were all sham! The people, surprised
By purple night after days of blind light

Cutting deep into their bodies of water and
Weeds. And the bruised handprints on crumbling

Walls. And dead strangers in every street.
And the sun with black grass stuffed in its mouth.

The Anatomy Lesson

If we will ever learn the correct
Order of the alphabets, we will then

Stop having to wear slopwork to school.
It comes down to many things: this is one:

Give a perch an inch and it will climb all
Over us and then be classified as a climbing

Perch, at least in the classroom. At table,
It wants some rather ebullient sauce and

Something green or leafy on the side. Taxonomy
Is anthropomorphic. It gives order to chaos.

It dilutes chaos and runs it down the funnel.
It is little more than medieval beast epics,

Expanding the scope of the world by giving accents
To geese or having dogs play ukuleles. Better

To analyze kinetic energy as a form of a defense
Mechanism. In any case, the principle is sound:

Do we become more taxon riding in a taxi, study
Water in the aquarium, say that clouds look good

Enough to drink, condemn cactus for choosing the desert,
Chase after rocks, expect the owl to speak Latin?

Like Tulipomania

Shakespeare didn't mention tulips in his plays.
He used twenty-five thousand words for color. In
1987 the buzz saw out my window neatly
Cuts a board in two and I've wondered whether
The stonemason next door feels particular to the first
Stone mortared into place. I've always
Thought it rude to be the first in line. But
The tulips bend together in the breeze. Call
Out a favorite color and it will appear.
The automatic sprinklers have been set
And are waiting for premonition to end.
The guests when they walk are made to wear straitjackets
To keep them from stuffing the vases in their
Bedrooms with tulips. Unlike praying mantises,
We have a human civility and don't usually
Sever heads of humans or flowers. How could
There be comments if we did? Please, no
Tulips as mementos—no pressing them in the telephone
Book under T, over time. Memory doesn't
Need to monitor eternity. Enough that there be
Some reminiscent hum of tulips expecting to open
At any moment, whether here and now or
Now and then, then and therefore, therefore and
Afterward, etc. There's no use patterning them
One spring like the mosaic in Sant' Apollinare in
Classe outside Ravenna, simply to out-Byzantine
The Byzantines. The muse does not belong in a
Museum. You do not mean monument, you
Mean demonstrate, speak with stones in your
Mouth if you can't speak. I only mention
This because I was fond of Demosthenes in
Grade school and almost swallowed the handful
Of lake-washed stones one summer evening. His
gums bled quickly. And who knows what he
Really said: "The tulips are too excitable"? I've
Heard the word before—it can make
One do things that one wouldn't normally do.

The Other Side of the Road

My clothes are circus tents trembling
In the wind. I sometimes hurry through

The streets, no thought of returning, and inspect
Even the dusty dying plants in the windows of

The dry cleaners, who have their phones off the hook
And must be making love. There are guesses and

There is picking the right horse, always. The sister
Of the moon is leaving, going back to the tobacco fields,

The stained teeth, the bulging cheeks of someone's
Desire. A Mexican hides a pepper behind his ear

Like a rocket. Raccoons open soda bottles for tourists,
Gratis. Somnambulism, my hoodlum cousin,

Once removed, now enters the house that it has
Been building and tearing down for thousands

Of years. See all the nails that hold
Everything in place: some inertia very like my

Body, which has a trace of form, like
Poison in good wine. Like other bodies shouting

Their shadows on the walls at night, when
The moon, again, is easiest to draw,

When it poses in the rose garden, at the lake.
Night pushes further as if on schedule, as if

The schedule means seclusion is something passed
Over quickly, while sleeping in hard beds, alone,

Or while sleeping all together, like the graves,
And while dreaming, seriously, something more to say.

Grammatical Existence

He always bought more than he could carry
And had complex thoughts about what was buried

Too deep inside him to explore. But he liked trouble.
It was the only time he could bet on subtle

Things making a difference: A certain look
Could mean the end of the world and he always took

Signs seriously, the way he held smells,
Supreme indicators of those things about to fall.

He once saw the world about to split in two.
He sat up in his chair and told the world to go

To hell. He was undivided in every way.
His calling was to spell his name very slowly, to say

The alphabet in his sleep, to take words for a walk,
To paste letters in the trees, and when called on, to talk.

Fly by Night

The lost world or one losing itself daily in a dark part
    Of this small room is in no danger
Of being found out. Choosing the jungle, banana leaves
    To set tea cups on, coconut
Milk delivered to our hut, breadfruit on all the menus.
    We're uncivilized and love
It. We can't count to ten anymore and refuse to try. We
    Can't walk now without touching
The ground at least once. Our songs flame up. Our cries
    Are torches to light this
Cave. Regrets for the fireless, the more or less quiescent-
    To-society crowd we've
Escaped from: tattle-tales, tutus, tuxedos, thrillers.

    The red and green
Birds of paradise in the front yard wake up the near-dead
    Every morning. An
Eyeful, at large. The night is collapsible, folded up
    Like a circus,
Sometimes, staid with its interminable history, how we
    Want it not to appear as
It does, so man-made, so out-there, telling the same
    Story. The night should come
On now, and only for a few minutes. Take a walk and
    Not find its way back.

There isn't anything to think of that can't erase itself
    Deeply so as to start
Over, so as to complicate with invisibility. Some books
    Should only be read at night,
And should be set afire when finished. The neighbor's
    Dog curls around its shadow,
The neighbor's cat carries its own at all times.
    The language school is burning tonight,
And the students inside don't know what to say. We
    Could tell them. We could talk
About the dull moon, the eclipse, the stable where
    The old horses sleep, the canary

In the coal mines, the rabbit in the trap, the swan
　　Swimming upside down,
The cemetery with its lights on, the day captured, taken
　　To the stake, given a last wish.

Katzenjammer

A Kleinschmidt is not a Blacksmith.
The former has only pounded tennis balls
With a tennis racket and quietly,
On grass courts, only the rhythmic
Plop plop, as if he were thumping his
Chest underwater. Most of the real blacksmiths
Have died, now that we are in the 20th
Century, and they've taken some of their loud
Sounds with them. They bent horseshoes—like
I have bent this line. They hammered
Out hot metal, and I have written
The words that say so. While I am doing
This in private, it's true my
Desk is a kind of anvil. I think
Of Hephaestus before his forge, fanning
Flames, bellowing, and how he would
Hobble home to light the fire in
Aphrodite's stove. He was a quiet
Man and listened only to the ringing
In his ears. There are now more
Smiths than any other English name.
They have made some noise. They
Have cut and pounded out a place.
John and Mary Smiths shout at each
Other, strike the hot iron and
Sizzle in a tub of cold water.
That chestnut tree that once had
Spread is dead, too. There is a subdivision
There now, with commuters, and the noise
They make all day is what I have to listen to.

Orchestrion

Or the Chinese chest of drawers taken
Straight from the train station here, to
The top of the stairs. It has other purposes
Than music; it will hold clothes, stacks
Of scarves, sweaters, perhaps not boxes jammed
With jewelry, but the ordinary clink of
Porcelain from Orvieto. Bottles in the bottom
Drawer ring themselves around the wine. In
Oxford is a staid shop that sells a bustle
That plays "God Save the Queen" when the wearer
Sits down. What contains its own container?
The dancers are moving again because of
The loud music next door. They had helped
Hoist the chest. They have legs made by lathes.
The flute is a woodwind but not wood wind, and
The *flautas* we had last night crunched.
The Border collie I used to have conducted sheep
Like Stokowski. He wrote the book on
The closed gate. The range of voices of cats in
Heat. Heavy-duty trucks pound across state
Lines and the radios are currently being
Tuned. Any dictionary will define song.
You have to find someone else to actually sing
It. Do you understand the position on substance:
A nightingale has none, is all song. If it sounds
As if these sentences were written to the metronome—
No. Beethoven was the first to use one, and he
Wrote for the orchestrion, a disembodied band.
Wittgenstein was known to be able to hum the complete
Brahms. He played clarinet in the World War I trenches,
While the stars danced and the soldiers advanced above
And below the mustard gas. There is no "player" in
Player piano. It is played upon, a field of sound.
Send us a sonargram, but what would it sound
Like. What would it sing that yet hasn't been sung?

Nomenclature

I don't know the real name of the saint,
Whose statue has been set on the hall
Chest. He was the senior left out of
The yearbook years ago. The years
Have gone—a little amnesia goes
A long way. The captions in
The scrapbooks are onomatopoetic, at
Best: Here is archetypal Eddie
With a masculine throw to home plate,
His first communion to last supper
Around the kitchen table that is groaning
With kitsch. The saint has a
Black licorice lacquer that is flaking,
Showing a lavender underneath—a sense
Of royalty, obliged to be *noblesse oblige.*
The poor pour in and the nameless are
Just shameless. And just any amnesty isn't
Appreciated: We long ago became those
Who've forgotten the forgotten. At her
Birth, a friend's parents wrote NO
NAME for her middle name, and she
Became —— Noname ——, like
Naomi, I guess. There seem to be
Many more nouns around these days.
The lavender saint is not amused
In the little hallway museum—
He wanted notoriety among
The *cognoscenti.* I've given him
A nickname, Saint-Saëns. Now
He can be a pronoun with a real
Antecedent. Now he can think of
The hall ceiling as heaven. No
Earthworm to cut trails in a wooden
Body, so suitable for a saint. No
Coelum for a soul or a heart, or
Entrails for divination. This saint
And I go back a long way. We were

Antonyms in another life. We answered
To the sound of our own names or just to
The sound of the wind, particular wind,
In the trees, elm, oak, maple—a wind
We can remember, a wind we can name.

A Note on the Author

Edward Kleinschmidt was born in Winona, Minnesota, in 1951. He received his B.A. from St. Mary's College (Minnesota) in 1974 and his M.A. from Hollins College in 1976.

His first book of poems, *Magnetism* (The Heyeck Press, 1987), received the 1988 Poetry Award from the San Francisco Bay Area Book Reviewers Association. His poetry, fiction, and essays have appeared in many journals and anthologies, including *The American Poetry Review, The Gettysburg Review, The Iowa Review, The Massachusetts Review, The New Yorker, North American Review, Poetry, Poetry Northwest,* among others.

Since 1981 he has taught English and creative writing at Santa Clara University. He lives in San Francisco.

THE
JUNIPER
PRIZE

This volume is the fifteenth recipient
of the Juniper Prize
presented annually by the
University of Massachusetts Press
for a volume of original poetry.
The prize is named in honor of
Robert Francis (1901–87),
who lived for many years at
Fort Juniper, Amherst, Massachusetts.